Casey's New Hat

Casey's New Hat

Tricia Gardella • Illustrated by Margot Apple

Houghton Mifflin Company
Boston 1997

For information about this and other Houghton Mifflin
trade and reference books and multimedia products,
visit The Bookstore at Houghton Mifflin on the World Wide
Web at http://www.hmco.com/trade/.

Manufactured in Singapore
TWP 10 9 8 7 6 5 4 3 2 1

The text of this book is set in 16 point Sabon.
The illustrations are color pencil, reproduced in full color.

Library of Congress Cataloging-in-Publication Data

Gardella, Tricia.
   Casey's new hat / Tricia Gardella; illustrated by Margot Apple.
   p. cm.
   Summary: Casey's hat is worn out, and despite searching all over the
ranch and in town, she can't find one that seems right until she sees Grandpa's
stained, dusty, crumpled old hat.
   ISBN 0-395-72035-4
   [1. Hats — Fiction. 2. Ranch life — Fiction. 3. Grandfathers — Fiction.]
I. Apple, Margot, ill. II. Title.
PZ7.G164Cas 1997
[E] — dc20 94-24408 CIP AC

For Michelle and Jodi, who DID get
their "just-right-hats" that Christmas
— T.G.

For Anna and Martha Dembek,
my little cowgirls in Montana
— M.A.

Casey pulled on her boots. She and
Dad were headed to town for supplies.
Where was her hat?

She looked on the shelf where her mother said it belonged. No hat.

She looked beneath her bed. Plastic horses, plastic cows, and Lincoln Logs to build corrals. No hat.

"Casey, are you coming?" Dad sounded ready.

Casey stood in the center of her room and slowly turned around. That's when she saw it. A red-and-white cord dangling over the edge of her toy basket.

Casey tugged her hat from under the horse trailer Grandpa had given her for her birthday. The trailer came with it.

"I'm coming," she called to Dad. Casey pushed out the crown and straightened the hat's brim. Then she settled the hat on her head and pushed the slide under her chin.

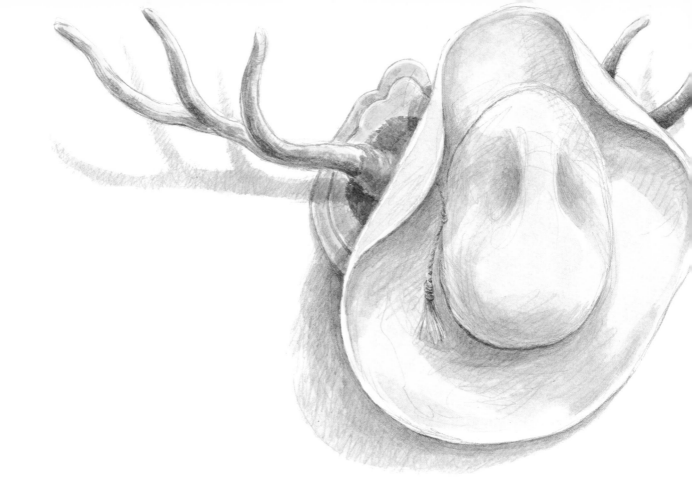

"Looks like you could use a new hat," Dad said.

Casey looked at herself in the hall mirror. She had worn this hat for as long as she could remember and it was getting a little tight.

"Maybe," she said. "But only if it's the right hat."

Casey and Dad went to the feed store first, to pick up grain for the horses. After the sacks were loaded, Dad led Casey to the back. Casey tried on big hats, and tall hats, and flat hats, and small hats.

"Nope," said Casey.

Next stop, the Clothes Horse, where Dad wanted to buy a new pair of jeans. Here they found hats with feathers, hats of leather, and hats that seemed to be made of lace.

Casey wrinkled her nose. "No way!"

When they stopped by the veterinary clinic for vaccine,
Dr. Steedman brought out a hat that a client had sent
from Australia.

"How about something like this?" he asked Casey.
The corks dangling in Casey's face made her laugh.
"They protect against flies," explained Dr. Steedman.

Back at the barn, Casey told the men about her hat search.
"Why didn't you ask me first? I have just the hat for you,"
said Carlos. But Carlos's hat felt like a cake on a plate,
balanced on Casey's head.

"Not quite," she said.

"How about mine?" asked Big Walt. This one was more like a bucket that covered clear to Casey's chin. Casey shook her head.

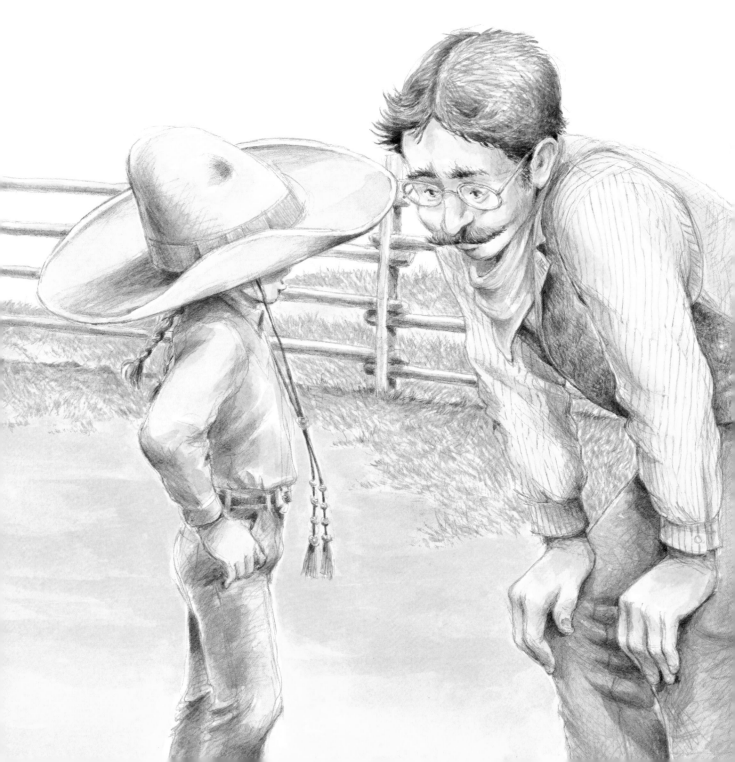

"Maybe one like mine," Grandpa teased. His brand-new Silverbelly 5X almost hurt Casey's eyes, it was so spotless. Casey thought about where she had found her hat this morning.

"Grandpa, your hat is way too fancy!"

"We'll look another day," Dad told her. "Right now I need you to go with Grandpa to feed those mares down by the creek."

Casey climbed into Grandpa's pickup. Grandpa's old hat was hanging in the rear window. The hat was crumpled and stained. It smelled of dust and cattle.

And it felt just right. Casey hopped down from the cab.
"That hat was old when you were born," Grandpa told
her. "That hat has been burned by the range fire. . . . That
hat nearly drowned in the river. . . . That hat has been
crushed by a stampede. . . ."

Casey rubbed her hand across the brim. "It's a perfect hat."